PINSTRIPES AND PENNANTS

THE ULTIMATE NEW YORK YANKEES FAN GUIDE

I0895870

BY BARRY WILNER

First Edition
First Printing, 2019

Book design by Sarah Taplin
Cover design by Sarah Taplin
Photographs ©: Julie Jacobson/AP Images, cover (left), cover (bottom right), 4, 8; Seth Wenig/AP Images, cover (top right); AP Images, 10, 18, 21, 22, 25, 31, 32, 36, 40, 43, 63, 71, 88, 94; Murray Becker/AP Images, 16, 92; Chris Bernacchi/AP Images, 27; Duane Burleson/AP Images, 28; Kyodo/AP Images, 38, 47; John Rooney/Images, 45; Chris O'Meara/AP Images, 48; JCH/AP Images, 52; Bill Kostroun/AP Images, 55, 82; Mark Lennihan/AP Images, 56, 96, 105; Richard Drew/AP Images, 60; Harry Harris/AP Images, 65; Winslow Townson/AP Images, 72; Abe Fox/AP Images, 75; Ray Stubblebine/AP Images, 79; Charles Krupa/AP Images, 86–87

Design Elements ©: Pixabay

Press Box Books, an imprint of Press Room Editions.

Library of Congress Control Number: 2018952197

ISBN:
978-1-63494-059-7 (paperback)
978-1-63494-071-9 (epub)
978-1-63494-083-2 (hosted ebook)

Distributed by North Star Editions, Inc.
2297 Waters Drive
Mendota Heights, MN 55120
www.northstareditions.com

Printed in the United States of America

TABLE OF CONTENTS

CHAPTER 1
Jeter's Farewell 5

CHAPTER 2
The Early Days 11

CHAPTER 3
The House That Ruth Built 19

CHAPTER 4
The Bronx Bombers 29

CHAPTER 5
Hurlers 41

CHAPTER 6
The Boss and the Managers 49

CHAPTER 7
Classic Games 57

CHAPTER 8
Baseball's Bitterest Rivalry 73

CHAPTER 9
Yankees Mount Rushmore 89

THE BEST OF THE REST 98
TIMELINE 100
YANKEES RECORDS 104
FOR MORE INFORMATION 106
PLACES TO VISIT 107
SELECT BIBLIOGRAPHY 108
INDEX 110
ABOUT THE AUTHOR 112

CHAPTER 1

JETER'S FAREWELL

Derek Jeter was always calm in the most pressure-filled times. So it was strange to see how he reacted after his final game at Yankee Stadium—one of the most memorable moments in the history of America's winningest franchise.

"It was sort of an out-of-body experience," Jeter said. "It was a weird range of emotions. I was just trying not to cry."

Lots of people at the stadium were shedding tears on the night of September 25, 2014, when Jeter played before them for the last time. His two decades as the New York Yankees' shortstop were filled with success: Rookie of the Year in 1996, 14 All-Star Game appearances, five Gold Gloves, and, most notably, five World Series championships.

Derek Jeter gave fans a night they'll never forget during his final game at Yankee Stadium.

PHIL RIZZUTO

Derek Jeter wasn't the first great Yankees shortstop. Phil Rizzuto was nicknamed "Scooter," and he lived up to the name. He scooted along the left side of the infield, gobbling up ground balls and spearing line drives at shortstop. And he scooted around the bases as he scored 877 runs in 13 seasons, ending in 1956.

But the Hall of Fame player was even more popular as an announcer. He often bragged about scooting from the broadcast booth to beat the traffic before the game ended. Among his favorite shticks were calling people "huckleberries" when they made errors; yelling "holy cow" when something wild happened; and speaking about his fear of lightning or his favorite restaurants.

Yankees fans ate it up.

On this night, even though it had been raining during the day, fans filled Yankee Stadium to say goodbye to one of the remarkable careers in modern sports. Many carried banners praising "The Captain," with one sign saying "Thanks 2 You," with the team's logo surrounding the "2" for Jeter's jersey number. Another offered "Derek, Thanks For Being The One We Could Always Turn 2."

As had become commonplace during his long career, Jeter did not disappoint.

Playing against the Baltimore Orioles, Jeter had a double and two runs batted in (RBIs). The Yankees were winning 5–2 when he took his position at shortstop in the top of the ninth. If that had been it, Jeter would have given the fans a typically memorable last game. The team's plan was indeed to remove Jeter, allowing for a standing ovation that might have lasted until October. Jeter knew that, and he could be seen wiping tears from his eyes during the inning.

"I've done a pretty good job controlling my emotions," Jeter said. "I try to hide them. I try to trick myself into not feeling those particular emotions. Today, I wasn't able to do it."

But Jeter's career wasn't over quite yet. Yankees closer David Robertson couldn't protect the lead. Soon the score was 5–5 heading into the bottom of the ninth, with Jeter due up third. That meant the Yankees faithful would get to see one more at-bat.

José Pirela led off with a single, and pinch runner Antoan Richardson was bunted to second. Up stepped Jeter, with the ground seeming to shake as everyone in the stands rose to their feet and cheered. Players in

Jeter celebrates after his walk-off hit gave the Yankees a victory in his final game at Yankee Stadium.

both dugouts stood by the railing to watch. What they saw was the stuff movies are made of.

Jeter swung at the first pitch from Evan Meek, using that inside-out swing that helped him to a career .310 batting average. The ball rocketed into right field, and Richardson stormed around third base. For a moment, all eyes turned away from Jeter to see the play at the plate.

SAFE!

As Yankees broadcaster John Sterling screamed "Yankees win" to his listeners, Jeter's teammates streamed out of the dugout. Former teammates had joined the team in the dugout. Among them were former manager Joe Torre and the other three members of the "Core Four"–Mariano Rivera, Jorge Posada, and Andy Pettitte–with whom Jeter had won four World Series.

Short of clinching a championship, rarely if ever was there such a wild scene in the ballpark in the Bronx. And it was far from over. After being mobbed by the other Yankees, Jeter paid tribute to the fans. He waved as he walked around the infield before stopping at–where else?–the shortstop part of the dirt.

Jeter kneeled, and he prayed.

"I basically just said, 'Thank you,'" Jeter explained, "because this is all I ever wanted to do. Not too many people have the opportunity to do it. It was above and beyond anything I dreamed."

Jeter then decided to play designated hitter, not shortstop, in the Yankees' final series at Boston. His reasoning made sense.

"I've only played shortstop for my entire career," he said, "and the last time I want to play it is tonight."

LIFEBUOY
CANADA DRY

CHAPTER 2

THE EARLY DAYS

When the New York Yankees joined the American League (AL) in 1903—well, they really didn't. At least not as the Yankees.

The team's history actually began two years earlier, in 1901 in Baltimore. When that team folded after two seasons, new owners stepped in. Some say the owners bought the team and moved it to New York. Others say they created a new team. Either way, a new major league team began play in New York in 1903, but it still wasn't called the Yankees. In fact, the team didn't have an official nickname right away.

Locals began calling them the Highlanders, because the team played games at Hilltop Park in upper Manhattan. Also, team president Joseph Gordon liked the reference to the British military unit known

Prior to making their home at Yankee Stadium, the Yankees played at the Polo Grounds from 1913 to 1922.

as the Gordon Highlanders. Soon enough, the team was officially the Highlanders.

Early on, Hilltop Park was basically a dump built near a swamp. For a while, it didn't even have grass in the outfield. The ballpark was not a comfortable place to watch baseball. Fans in those days were allowed to stand in back of the outfielders and even in foul territory, so approximately 25,000 people could watch big games.

In addition to the name, the Highlanders were hardly recognizable as forerunners of the Yankees teams to come. During those first 10 seasons, the team went 734–759 overall, and three times it finished second in the AL. But more often they were more like the Lowlanders, finishing far out of contention. Among the team's stars were future Hall of Famers Willie Keeler and Jack Chesbro. Telling them apart wasn't always easy, though. Numbers weren't added to the team's uniforms until 1929.

In 1911, the more popular New York Giants saw their nearby stadium, the Polo Grounds, burned down, so the Highlanders shared Hilltop Stadium with the Giants. The sharing continued in 1913, as the Giants and Highlanders both played at the rebuilt

Polo Grounds. In addition to moving, the Highlanders were finally renamed the Yankees, a nickname many fans had already adopted.

Things weren't much better at the Polo Grounds for the next six seasons, five of which the Yankees finished with a losing record. But in 1919, with Miller Huggins as manager, they went 80–59 to finish third in the AL. Future Hall of Famer Frank "Home Run" Baker anchored the lineup, hitting 10 dingers—a good number at the time. Meanwhile, pitcher Bob Shawkey won 20 games and saved five. One player who didn't quite pan out was outfielder George Halas. But after leaving the team he did just fine in football. Halas went on to help found the Chicago Bears and the National Football League.

Everything changed for the Yankees in 1920. That's when they bought a promising slugger named Babe Ruth from the Boston Red Sox. That year, Ruth took advantage of the Polo Grounds' short fences in left and right field to hit an astounding 54 home runs. Prior to Ruth, no player had hit more than 27 homers in a season. The team also featured Bob Meusel, another standout outfielder, as well as first baseman Wally Pipp. On the mound, 20-game winners in Shawkey and Carl Mays led the way. With 95 wins, the Yankees placed third in the AL, and they drew 1,289,422 fans, more than double the number from the previous year.

Still, they'd never been in the postseason. That changed in 1921.

The lineup was good, though not yet the historically good "Murderer's Row" that would come later. Ruth kept up his incredible power hitting with 59 homers, and Meusel had 24, but no one else had more than nine. Still, the Yankees had enough firepower to win 98 games. With no playoffs yet, the team with the most wins claimed the first pennant and went straight to the World Series. There, the Yankees' opponent from the National League (NL) was none other than the crosstown Giants.

The first Subway Series got off to a great start for the Yankees as their aces, Mays and Waite Hoyt, threw shutouts. But then the Giants' bats woke up.

In those days, it took five victories to win the Series. The Giants won twice to even the series before Hoyt beat them again in Game 5. However, the Yankees were in trouble. Ruth was injured with an infected elbow. Sportswriting legend Grantland Rice wrote that Babe's arm was so swollen, it "looked like an elephant's thigh." The Giants won 8–5 in Game 6. But without their star player, the Yankees struggled to put runs on the board the rest of the way. The pitchers did their best, with Mays allowing just two runs in Game 7 and Hoyt giving up one unearned run in Game 8. But without Ruth, the Yankees lost both. Still, even in defeat, the Yankees made it known they would be a force—a hurricane-type force.

That hurricane would blow from a new home in 1923. Owner Jacob Ruppert had dreamed of his own ballpark, and in 1923, Yankee Stadium opened directly across the Harlem River from the Polo Grounds. Fans could walk across a bridge from one venue to the other.

During the next six seasons, with first baseman Lou Gehrig, infielder Tony Lazzeri, outfielder Earle Combs, and pitcher Herb Pennock joining the roster, the Yankees won four pennants. And in 1923, they won their first World Series. That title came against the now-hated Giants, who had also beaten the Yankees in the '22 Series.

Few teams have had it all quite like the 1927 Yankees. That year, everything came together on what many consider the greatest team in baseball history.

Infielder Tony Lazzeri was key to five of the Yankees teams that won the World Series during the 1920s and 1930s.

"Those fellows not only beat you, but they tear your hearts out," said Washington Senators first baseman Joe Judge.

Ruth led an utterly dominant lineup. He slugged 60 homers, which would be the record until 1961. And amazingly, his 165 RBIs didn't even lead the team: Gehrig had 173. Combs, Ruth, and Gehrig each scored at least 137 runs, with the team totaling 976 runs. Home runs? The Yankees launched 158; the other seven teams in the AL combined for 281. And of the Yankees' regular batters, only third baseman Joe Dugan (.269) and catcher Pat Collins (.275) hit below .300. It was no surprise the lineup became known as Murderer's Row.

But this was not just an offensive powerhouse. Opponents scored only 605 runs, which was the fewest in the AL by more than 100.

After going 110–44 to win the pennant by 19 games, the Yankees toyed with the Pittsburgh Pirates in the World Series. Even though Pittsburgh had five future Hall of Famers, New York swept.

The Yankees were on their way to becoming the greatest dynasty in sports.

CHAPTER 3

THE HOUSE THAT RUTH BUILT

When Jacob Ruppert and Tillinghast L'Hommedieu Huston bought the Yankees in 1915, the team shared the Polo Grounds with the New York Giants. This wasn't the worst situation. The Yankees had gotten out of the dingy Hilltop Park. And the Yankees often drew more fans than the Giants, who were the ballpark's main tenant.

Naturally, the Giants disliked that. So in 1922, when the Yanks' lease ended, the Giants told them they were no longer welcome. This presented Ruppert, a former congressman and colonel in the National Guard, with his opportunity to build the team its own park.

Yankee Stadium was a revolution when it opened in 1923, as it was the first stadium to feature three decks of seating.

Rupert, by now the sole owner, responded by buying land across the Harlem River in the Bronx, within walking distance of the Polo Grounds. Yankee Stadium opened on April 18, 1923, with 58,000 seats, three decks—a first in baseball—and a facade atop the third deck considered the venue's most special feature.

Opening Day saw New York Governor Al Smith throw out the first ball. Bands played to entertain the full house, many of whom paid all of $1.10 to get in—a fairly expensive price in those days. Hardly surprising, they got their thrill from Babe Ruth. The Babe's three-run homer was the difference in a 4–1 victory over Boston. When Ruth rounded third base, he took off his cap and saluted the crowd as he trotted home.

That wasn't the last time Ruth thrilled fans in the ballpark, which led fans to nickname the stadium "The House That Ruth Built." And Ruth was far from the only Yankees star to thrive there.

There have been three versions of Yankee Stadium. The first lasted until 1973, when it was remodeled, though not changed much. That second version lasted through 2008. The following year, an entirely new ballpark opened across the street from the original.

The original proved to be a welcome home for the parade of stars who called it home through the

Babe Ruth was one of the first stars to call Yankee Stadium home. His success led to fans calling the stadium "The House That Ruth Built."

years. For powerful left-handed hitters such as Ruth, Lou Gehrig, Yogi Berra, and switch-hitter Mickey Mantle, the short right field porch at less than 300 feet was an easy target. But there were also deep alleys in left-center and right-center. Dead center once was 490 feet, though it was later reduced to 461 feet. So the Yankees always needed a fast, smart, alert, strong-armed player out there. Of course, they had them with players such as Earl Combs, Joe DiMaggio, and Mantle.

What the Yankees—and every other baseball team—didn't have through 1928 was numbers on

Outfielder Mickey Mantle hit many of his 536 home runs to Yankee Stadium's short right field porch.

their uniforms. The Cleveland Indians experimented with numbers in 1916 but then dropped them. Ruppert wanted his club to be the first to have them permanently, and he planned for it in 1929. Then Mother Nature interfered. New York's home opener was rained out, but Cleveland played as planned. That meant the Indians got to unveil their numbered jerseys first, this time permanently.

The Yankees used logic in handing out numbers, with Ruth getting No. 3 because he batted third, Gehrig No. 4 because he was the cleanup hitter, and so on.

No baseball team, however, has come close to the volume of retired numbers that the Yankees have. No Yankees player will ever wear the numbers 1 through 10 again. Those retired numbers represent a who's who in iconic Yankees history: 1 (Billy Martin), 2 (Derek Jeter), 3 (Babe Ruth), 4 (Lou Gehrig), 5 (Joe DiMaggio), 6 (Joe Torre), 7 (Mickey Mantle), 8 (Yogi Berra and Bill Dickey), 9 (Roger Maris), and 10 (Phil Rizzuto).

Those uniforms worn proudly at Yankee Stadium have remained almost unchanged: white with blue pinstripes. However, the signature feature didn't actually start in New York. The Chicago Cubs were the first to have pinstripes, which they had on their road uniforms. The pinstripes also didn't catch on right away in New York. In 1912, the Highlanders had

NEW YORK, NEW YORK

Frank Sinatra, the legendary singer, is often identified with New York City. So it made sense in 1980 when Yankees owner George Steinbrenner ordered that Sinatra's version of "New York, New York" be played at the end of games. Following the 1996 World Series, a six-game win over Atlanta, fans stood in celebration and loudly sang along with Sinatra's recording.

uniforms with black pinstripes. But New York lost 102 games that season and dropped the pinstripes. Three years later, in 1915, the pinstripes were back, this time in blue. That has never changed.

"(It's the) history," Jeter said. "That's not being disrespectful to any other team, but you say pinstripes and the first thing that comes to most people's mind is the Yankees. There's just so much history there and tradition, it makes it special for us as players.

"It's always cool. You put it on before every game and you feel special. It's different for me when I put on a different uniform: Team USA, the All-Star Game during workouts, minor league rehab games. It just feels funny, you know what I mean? The pinstripes, they just feel right, I guess."

The interlocking "NY," as famous as the pinstripes, was on the jersey from 1909 to 1917 and then returned in 1936. Oddly, Ruth never wore that logo on his Yankees jersey. In 1922, the logo made its way onto the cap in navy blue and white, where it remained.

Although the look the players wear hasn't changed much, the look of where they play certainly has. Yes, it's often called the "Home of Champions," and the bleachers remain a nifty place to watch. But both newer versions of Yankee Stadium had major changes.

For more than a century, fans have been able to identify the Yankees by their famous pinstripes.

In 1973 and '74, while the Yankees shared Shea Stadium with the Mets, the 50-year-old ballpark in the Bronx was remodeled. Many steel columns that partially blocked views were removed. Sight lines were improved, and a huge scoreboard was built behind the bleachers—with a copy of the facades on top. For fan comfort, three escalator towers were built.

The feel of the "new" stadium didn't change, though—especially when the Yankees started winning again. In 1976, they claimed their first pennant in 12 years. Although they lost in the World Series to the

Cincinnati Reds, they won the championship the next two seasons and added four more from 1996 to 2000.

By 2008, though, it was time for a truly new ballpark. Other teams had grand stadiums with luxury boxes and restaurants, huge high-tech scoreboards, and more comfortable seats. As the Yankees' latest home rose across the street to the tune of $1.6 billion, Jeter was their final batter in the old Yankee Stadium.

"For all of us up here, it's a huge honor to put this uniform on every day and come out here and play," Jeter said. "And every member of this organization, past and present, has been calling this place

MONUMENT PARK

There are 38 men honored with either a monument or a plaque beyond the center field wall at Yankee Stadium. The six monuments are for Babe Ruth, Lou Gehrig, Joe DiMaggio, Miller Huggins, Mickey Mantle, and George Steinbrenner. There's also a monument in remembrance of the victims of the September 11 terrorist attacks.

Plaques also honor dignitaries Nelson Mandela, Pope Paul VI, Pope John Paul II, and Pope Benedict XVI, all of whom visited the stadium.

The Yankees opened the new Yankee Stadium on a high note in 2009 with a World Series crown.

home for 85 years. There's a lot of tradition, a lot of history, and a lot of memories. Now the great thing about memories is you're able to pass it along from generation to generation.

"And although things are going to change next year, we're going to move across the street, there are a few things with the New York Yankees that never change–it's pride, it's tradition, and most of all, we have the greatest fans in the world."

True to his word, Jeter and the Yankees opened the current Yankee Stadium with another special season that ended in their 27th World Series title.

NEW Y

CHAPTER 4

THE BRONX BOMBERS

It's not clear who nicknamed the Yankees the "Bronx Bombers," but the name sure made sense. After all, the team has played in that New York City borough since 1923. And during that time, the Yankees have had some of the greatest power hitters in baseball.

It began with Babe Ruth and Lou Gehrig, then continued with Joe DiMaggio. After that, it was Mickey Mantle, Roger Maris, Reggie Jackson, and Alex Rodriguez. And now, Gary Sanchez, Giancarlo Stanton, and 2017 AL Rookie of the Year Aaron Judge carry on the tradition. Amazingly, Judge hit 52 home runs in his rookie season. How high could he go?

With 33 homers in 2017, Gary Sanchez helped usher in a new era of power hitting at Yankee Stadium.

"I hate to put a number on him," teammate Brett Gardner said of Judge. "But we all know how physically gifted he is and how big and strong he is. So nothing would surprise me, really."

For pull hitters, Yankee Stadium can be heavenly. The distances are short down both lines. But in all three versions of the ballpark, center field and its gaps have been like Grand Canyons. Yet the Yankees always have found, well, bombers.

Here are some of the most famous sluggers and the iconic home runs they have hit.

BABE RUTH

Argue all you want whether it's true, but the Babe's "called shot" is a terrific story.

It was 1932, and the Yankees traveled to Wrigley Field to face the Chicago Cubs in Game 3 of the World Series. New York had won the first two games at home. Then Ruth opened the third game with a three-run homer in the first inning. However, Chicago caught up. The game was tied 4–4 when Ruth came up in the fifth.

Players in the Cubs' dugout were teasing Ruth. With the count 2–2, Ruth stepped out of the batter's box and—so it is told—pointed two fingers toward

Before Babe Ruth came along, few players hit double-digit home runs in a season.

center field. On the next pitch, he sent the ball rocketing into the bleachers in center field.

Afterward, Ruth claimed he called his shot. Cubs pitcher Charlie Root said the Babe was showing there were two strikes on him. Whatever the truth, Babe's homer helped the Yankees sweep the World Series.

With a then-record 60 home runs in 1927 and 714 for his career, Ruth set the standard by which all future power hitters are judged.

Lou Gehrig hit nearly 500 home runs in his illustrious career as a Yankee.

LOU GEHRIG

That same 1932 season, the Iron Horse hit four round-trippers in one game.

On June 3 against the Philadelphia Athletics, Gehrig's four homers—and Tony Lazzeri's cycle (single, double, triple, homer)—powered the Yankees to a 20–13 win. Gehrig homered in the first, fourth, fifth (right after Ruth hit one), and seventh, becoming the first player since the 1890s to knock out four in a game. And he almost got another: In the ninth, his long fly ball to deepest center field was caught 460 feet away. Those homers were four of 493 he hit in his career.

JOE DIMAGGIO

One of his nicknames was "Joltin' Joe," and as a rookie in 1936, he earned that. DiMaggio missed about a month at the start of the season with a foot injury. Yet he still managed to hit 29 homers that year, a team mark for rookies that stood until Judge came along.

During his record 56-game hitting streak in 1941 that no one has come close to touching, DiMaggio hit 15 homers. For his career, he had 361 homers, despite missing three full seasons while in the military.

MICKEY MANTLE

Probably the best switch hitter in baseball history, Mantle could send balls into orbit from either side of the plate.

At Washington's Griffith Park in 1953, Mantle hit a right-handed shot off Chuck Stobbs that observers claimed would have easily left the stadium on a fly and gone who knows how far? Instead, it hit an advertisement sign on the football scoreboard, yet still soared across Fifth Street before landing in a backyard of a house.

Immediately, Yankees publicist Red Patterson raced there to measure how far from the stadium's outside wall the ball landed. The number: 565 feet.

Some claim the term *tape measure home run* was invented that day.

ROGER MARIS

Maris was a terrific outfielder with a strong arm. Until he got to the Yankees, he was a good but not great power hitter. In 1961, though, it was bombs away as he set the single-season home run record and won his second straight AL Most Valuable Player (MVP) Award.

Maris had hit 59 homers heading into the final week of the schedule. However, his chase for 60 wasn't that popular with New Yorkers. They loved the legend of the Babe, who hit 60 in a 154-game season in 1927. The fans didn't feel the same way about Maris, playing in a 162-game season. And if anyone was to match Ruth, they preferred the more popular Mantle. But the Mick was sidelined in late September by an infection.

Maris slumped as he got closer to Ruth, admitting the pressure got to him. But with six days left in the season, Maris drilled Baltimore's Jack Fisher's pitch into the right field stands for his 60th. The crowd stood and cheered until Maris did a rare thing, stepping out of the dugout to wave.

It took until the last of 162 games for him to hit number 61. Boston's Tracy Stallard allowed it, a drive to right field that a 19-year-old truck driver from Brooklyn, Sal Durante, caught.

"As soon as Roger hit it, I jumped on my seat and reached as high as I could," he said. "It hit right in the palm of my hand."

Afterward, Durante offered Maris the ball, but the player had other ideas. "He said, 'No, you keep the baseball and make yourself some money,'" Durante recalled. "That's the kind of guy Roger was, a very thoughtful, generous man." And also the new one-season home run king.

REGGIE JACKSON

Jackson was such a big star in Oakland and then New York that a candy bar was named after him. But he's most remembered in the Bronx for the three homers he hit in a clinching Game 6 of the 1977 World Series, tying another one of Ruth's records.

Following Ruth's example, Reggie Jackson put on a show in the 1977 World Series when he hit three homers in Game 6.

Playing the Los Angeles Dodgers, Jackson sent Burt Hooton's pitch far into the stands in the fourth inning. Then he hit another home run against Elias Sosa in the fifth. He finished the hat trick of homers against Dodgers knuckleballer Charlie Hough in the eighth.

All three came on the first pitch.

"If you were watching TV, I know you saw me holding up one finger, then two, then three," Jackson wrote in the *New York Daily News*. "I was doing that for my mom. I knew the camera was on me, so I said, 'Hi Mom,' and I held up one finger. Then I hit the next one, and said, 'Hi Mom,' and held up two. Then, the third one, and I said, 'Hi mom,' and held up three."

ALEX RODRIGUEZ

Alex Rodriguez had his ups and downs in a 22-year career, including allegations of using performance-enhancing drugs. Those drugs may have played a role in his massive home run totals. Five times, A-Rod led the AL in long balls, including twice as a Yankee.

Of his 696 career homers, 351 came as a Yankee. The strangest might have been in the 2009 World Series against the Philadelphia Phillies. It was the first time instant replay was used in a Series game.

Rodriguez's drive to right field was ruled a double. The ball had slammed off a TV camera down the line. A-Rod motioned to the umpires he thought it was a home run. The umps weren't sure, so they got together, looked at a TV monitor, and changed it to a homer.

Alex Rodriguez blasts a two-run homer against the Philadelphia Phillies in Game 3 of the 2009 World Series.

"I think it woke our offense up a little bit," Rodriguez said. "It felt really good, and it was a little weird to have the first home run and the replay and the whole nine yards. But two big runs for us early on."

AARON JUDGE

All rise.

When outfielder Aaron Judge came to the plate during his 2017 AL Rookie of the Year season, fans stood. Yes, they were aware how people in courtrooms rise when the judge enters. But more often they got out of their seats to watch Judge plant one of his 52 home runs into the stands.

Judge became the centerpiece of a lineup some called the "Modern Murderer's Row," which also included Gary Sanchez, Giancarlo Stanton, Didi Gregorious, and Gleyber Torres. Judge's homers usually went beyond 400 feet, some sailing into the section at Yankee Stadium called the "Judge's Chambers," where fans dressed in long black robes like you'd see in a courtroom.

"It's pretty cool," Judge said. "When you come to a game, it's supposed to be fun for the players and fans. I think it turned out great."

CHAPTER 5

HURLERS

Although called the Bronx Bombers, the Yankees have sent hundreds of good pitchers—and many great ones, including Hall of Famers—to the mound.

They've had multiple Cy Young Award winners since the top pitching honor was created in 1956. They've had powerful fastballers (Goose Gossage, Ron Guidry, Roger Clemens), crafty left-handers (Whitey Ford, Sparky Lyle, Luis Arroyo), and tireless righties (Catfish Hunter, Herb Pennock, Waite Hoyt, Spud Chandler).

It didn't matter whether they were starters or relievers, and it didn't matter whether they threw junk (Arroyo and the screwball) or darts (Mariano Rivera's assortment of fastballs). They won. So did the Yankees.

Ron Guidry overpowered hitters during the 1970s and 1980s thanks to a blazing fastball.

Ford won 10 World Series games and six championships. He was the MVP of the 1961 World Series—quite an achievement, considering that was one of the top Yankees hitting squads ever. Ford allowed six hits in two games, and no runs.

That was Ford at his best. He threw 45 shutouts in his 16 seasons in New York. In all, his .690 winning percentage was tops for any post-1900 pitcher in the Hall of Fame.

Ford got a late start toward Cooperstown, serving two years in the military before joining the rotation in 1953. He was the Yankees' ace for a dozen seasons; in 1955, he threw consecutive one-hitters.

RON GUIDRY

The left-hander known as "Louisiana Lightning" is not in the Hall of Fame, but his 1978 season is among the best ever. Even though he was slender at 160 pounds, Guidry could throw a baseball through a hurricane. He also had a nasty slider something like Sparky Lyle's. When he won the Cy Young Award in 1978, Guidry was 25–3 with nine shutouts, a 1.74 ERA, and 16 complete games. He fanned 248 batters and allowed a mere 53 earned runs.

Whitey Ford led the Yankees during a stretch that saw New York win six World Series in the 1950s and 1960s.

One more stunning stat: Ford allowed only 30 stolen bases in his entire career.

"I don't care what the situation was, how high the stakes were," Mickey Mantle said. "The bases could be loaded and the pennant riding on every pitch, it never bothered Whitey. He pitched his game. Cool. Craft. Nerves of steel."

One of Ford's biggest helpers was Arroyo. Relief pitchers were no big deal for most teams back then.

But when Arroyo had 29 saves in 1961, they became a big deal.

Talk about craft: the 5-foot-8 lefty mastered the screwball, which was basically a curveball that broke the opposite way. And while Arroyo's Yankees career was short (four years), his impact on pitching was massive. After his success, other teams began training pitchers to be relievers. That led to some of New York's most brilliant bullpen artists: Lyle, Gossage, and Rivera.

Lyle was known as much for his locker room antics—he liked to jump onto other players' birthday cakes and stick goldfish in the team water cooler—as for his pitching skills. He won the 1977 Cy Young Award as the Yankees won the World Series. His go-to pitch was a slider that, when it was dancing in the air, was almost impossible to hit.

Gossage was the opposite: all heat. He joined the Yankees in 1978 as they went to a lefty-righty closer combination. Standing 6-foot-3 and with a mustache that looked almost as long, Gossage was scary on the mound. Want proof? In 1980, he struck out more than one batter per inning—103 in 99 innings.

New York's next shutdown reliever was converted starter Dave Righetti. In 1983, Righetti threw the

Though Sparky Lyle was fun-loving off the field, his pitching ability was no joke, especially in 1977.

first Yankees no-hitter in 27 years. By '84 he was the Yankees' closer, and two years later had 46 saves, a team record until Rivera arrived.

Rivera, too, began his career as a starter. After one so-so season in 1995, he was switched to the bullpen. Rivera never started another game, but boy did he finish them. Entering to the Metallica song "Enter Sandman," Rivera put opposing batters to sleep with his assortment of pitches. The most lethal was a split-fingered fastball called a "cutter." It seemed to have the bottom drop out when it reached home plate. As Rivera piled up a record 652 saves in 18 seasons as a reliever, his favorite pitch began to spread throughout the majors.

"When I broke into the big leagues," says teammate Alex Rodriguez, "I can't remember more than a few guys who threw the cutter. Now almost every pitcher you face has a cutter or some fashion of it. And we have Mo to blame for it."

> "Now almost every pitcher you face has a cutter or some fashion of it. And we have Mo to blame for it."
>
> —Alex Rodriguez

When Rivera left the game in 2013, batters throughout the major leagues sighed in relief.

Using his signature cut fastball, Mariano Rivera picked up 652 saves during his career as Yankees closer.

CHAPTER 6

THE BOSS AND THE MANAGERS

They called him the Boss, and George Steinbrenner took that role seriously. Maybe too seriously: Ask the 15 men who either resigned or were hired and fired as manager by the Yankees owner. That includes Billy Martin holding the job five times. Bob Lemon, Gene Michael, and Lou Piniella each held it twice.

Steinbrenner took over a team with a long tradition of great managers, including some of baseball's finest of all time. Miller Huggins, Joe McCarthy, and Casey Stengel all went to the Hall of Fame. Each coached some of baseball's all-time great players, too.

George Steinbrenner was a notoriously hard boss to please during his time as Yankees owner.

Huggins was in charge of "Murderer's Row," which began the Pinstripe Dynasty in the 1920s with Babe Ruth and Lou Gehrig. He led the team to a 1,067–719 record and won three championships. McCarthy had Joe DiMaggio, Bill Dickey, Tommy Henrich, and Red Ruffing among his stars, and he led his teams to a 1,460–867 record and seven World Series titles. Stengel, meanwhile, had the likes of Mickey Mantle, Yogi Berra, and Whitey Ford. He led those players to a 1,149–696 record and seven Series rings, tying McCarthy for the most championships of all time.

Steinbrenner's arrival brought in a new era. A shipbuilder from Cleveland, Steinbrenner bought the Yankees in 1973 for $8.7 million. By 2015, the team was worth $3.2 billion.

By all measures, Steinbrenner was a very good owner. He spent money on the team, bringing in such high-priced players as Reggie Jackson, Catfish Hunter, and Goose Gossage, all future Hall of Famers. He persuaded New York City to help pay to remodel Yankee Stadium. He demanded excellence, and usually got it, winning seven World Series.

"Nobody wanted to win as much as George, and he demanded the same of everyone he worked with," said

Harvey Greene, who spent four seasons as Yankees publicity director before joining the Miami Dolphins. "It was tough, but I learned a lot. And while I don't know if I'd want to do it again, I was grateful for the lessons I learned working for him. It really prepared me for working under (successful football coaches) Don Shula, Jimmy Johnson, Nick Saban, and Bill Parcells."

If Steinbrenner was hard on front office folks, he could be impossible with managers. Bill Virdon, Dick Howser, and Bob Lemon, were three easygoing guys. All had run-ins with the Boss.

Some managers stood up to Steinbrenner. Berra, Piniella, and Dallas Green didn't back down; all were fired.

Nothing, though, approached Steinbrenner's relationship with the excitable Martin. A popular Yankees infielder as a player, Martin was known for never backing down on the field. He took that approach to managing, first with the Minnesota Twins, Detroit Tigers, and Texas Rangers. Then, in the middle of the 1975 season, Martin was fired by the Rangers and quickly hired by the Boss.

Steinbrenner told Martin he expected only one thing: a winner.

Winning two AL pennants and a World Series wasn't enough to keep Billy Martin on George Steinbrenner's good side.

And in 1976, Martin led the Yankees to the AL pennant. The next year, they beat the Los Angeles Dodgers in the World Series. Martin and Steinbrenner were buddy-buddy.

By July 1978, things turned rotten between them. The Yankees, with the best lineup in baseball, were struggling. Martin was feuding with star outfielder Jackson, who had cost the team a game by trying to bunt against Martin's orders.

When Martin said some nasty things about Jackson and Steinbrenner, he was fired. But Steinbrenner had second thoughts. Days after getting rid of Martin, the Boss had legendary stadium announcer Bob Sheppard tell the sellout crowd at the team's Old Timers' Day that Martin would return to manage two years later in 1980, replacing Lemon.

In '78 Lemon guided the Yankees to one of their greatest comebacks and championships. But he didn't make it to 1980. Sixty-five games into 1979, Lemon was out and Martin was back in.

That lasted 95 games; then he was canned again. Martin headed to Oakland, where he spent three seasons before being fired–and Steinbrenner quickly grabbed him back.

You must know what happened next. Martin lasted one season and then he was promoted to the front office as Berra became manager. And when Berra was fired by the Boss during the 1985 season, in stepped Martin for the fourth time.

He wasn't done. Nor was Steinbrenner, who replaced Martin with Piniella for the 1986 and '87 seasons. When Piniella wanted out, guess who Steinbrenner turned to–again. Martin went 40–28

JOE TORRE

An excellent player with three ballclubs, Joe Torre led the NL in hitting in 1971, when he was NL MVP. But he made his biggest mark as a manager, being elected to the Hall of Fame in 2014.

As Yankees manager, he oversaw the early careers of Derek Jeter, Andy Pettitte, Bernie Williams, and Jorge Posada. He was behind Mariano Rivera becoming a relief pitcher. And, somehow, he got along with the Boss for a dozen seasons.

in 1988 before being replaced by, yep, Piniella. That was the last stint as manager for Martin, who died in a car accident the next year.

Surprisingly, Steinbrenner finally found managers he wouldn't feud with and fire. Buck Showalter lasted four years; then Joe Torre spent 12 seasons in charge, winning four World Series.

When Torre left after 2007, Joe Girardi was hired and won a championship in his second season. With Steinbrenner, if you won, at least you had a chance to hold on to your job. One year after that 2009 championship, Steinbrenner died. However, his family still owns the team.

Joe Torre (left) was one of the few managers who avoided being fired by Yankees owner George Steinbrenner (right).

24

CHAPTER 7

CLASSIC GAMES

When you've been around for more than a century, and had the unmatchable success the Yankees have had, you'll own a long and proud list of classic victories and stunning performances. Here are some of the best.

A WILD RIDE (1996 PLAYOFFS)

Going into the 1996 postseason, the Yankees hadn't won a championship since 1978. Three magical events ended that title slump.

At Baltimore in Game 1 of the AL Championship Series (ALCS), the Orioles led 4–3. Then Derek Jeter hit a fly ball to right field in the eighth inning. Right fielder Tony Tarasco appeared ready to make the catch. Instead, 12-year-old Yankees fan Jeffrey Maier

After going 18 years without a title, the Yankees finally broke through against the Atlanta Braves in the 1996 World Series.

leaned over from the front row and caught it above Tarasco's head.

Umpire Rich Garcia signaled a home run; replays clearly showed Maier had interfered. That meant the batter should have been out. But umpires couldn't use replay, so the Yankees won the game, and after five tough contests, they eliminated the O's.

Next up was the World Series against the Atlanta Braves, with one of the all-time best pitching staffs. They won the first two games at Yankee Stadium, 12–1 and 4–0. Things looked bleak for the New Yorkers as they headed to Atlanta.

But David Cone won Game 3 for New York. The next night, in Game 4, the Yankees fell behind 6–0. They fought back to make it 6–3, forcing Atlanta to bring in closer Mark Wohlers in the eighth inning. Not a good idea.

Following two singles, supersub Jim Leyritz homered to left to make the score 6–6. The Yankees were refreshed and went on to win 8–6.

"It was pretty important, but it wasn't (to win) the World Series," Leyritz said. "Now that I've hit this home run, I hope we go on to win the Series so it will be even bigger."

Bingo. The Yankees won the next two, celebrating on their home field after Game 6–led by Wade Boggs. The third baseman hadn't won a ring in his previous 14 seasons. So when this one was clinched, Boggs hopped aboard a horse being ridden around the field by a city policeman.

"I didn't even realize what I was doing until I was halfway up there," said Boggs. "I'm deathly afraid of horses. I just did it. It felt great. This is what I've been waiting for."

BYE-BYE BABE (JUNE 13, 1948)

It was a sad sight when Babe Ruth said goodbye at the ballpark he made famous.

On June 13, 1948, celebrating 25 years at Yankee Stadium, the team invited many of its former stars to the game. Ruth, of course, was the biggest of them all, even though he was ill and slightly bent over while leaning on a bat when introduced to the full house.

"There have been so many lovely things said about me today that I'm glad to have had the opportunity to thank everybody," Ruth said. "Thank you."

Ruth died two months later.

With 18 strikeouts on June 17, 1978, Ron Guidry set a new standard in Yankees dominance.

LOUISIANA LIGHTNING (VS. CALIFORNIA ANGELS, JUNE 17, 1978)

Ron Guidry's fastball earned him the nickname Louisiana Lightning. Yet many opponents would say it was the mix of other pitches that made Guidry impossible to hit.

In his historic 1978 Cy Young–winning season, Guidry's masterpiece was when he fanned 18 Angels in a 4–0 four-hitter. Every Angels batter struck out at least once.

"If you saw that pitching too often," said Angels first baseman Joe Rudi, who fanned four times, "there would be a lot of guys doing different jobs."

JETER'S FLIP (AT OAKLAND ATHLETICS, 2001 AL DIVISION SERIES)

Even when he popped up out of nowhere, Derek Jeter somehow was where he belonged.

In Game 3 of the 2001 AL Division Series, with the Yankees down two games to none, they led Oakland 1–0 in the bottom of the seventh inning. Then Terrence Long doubled down the right field line.

The A's Jeremy Giambi tried to score from first base. That looked like it'd be no problem when outfielder Shane Spencer overthrew both cutoff men. The ball was bouncing between the pitcher's mound and first base line when Jeter—remember, he's a shortstop—grabbed the ball and flipped it backhanded to catcher Jorge Posada.

Giambi didn't slide, Posada made the tag on his leg, and the Yankees held on. They wound up beating Oakland in five games, then Seattle in five before heading to the World Series.

SORRY, RED SOX (VS. BOSTON RED SOX, OCTOBER 1–2, 1949)

Beating your top rival is always sweet. Doing so to win the pennant is even sweeter. On the first two days of

October 1949, the Yankees needed a pair of wins over visiting Boston to edge the Red Sox for the AL title.

Johnny Lindell's homer won the first game 5–4. Then New York had to beat Ellis Kinder, who'd won 15 straight decisions as a starter. The Yankees came out on top, 5–3. It would be 19 years before Red Sox owner Tom Yawkey would visit Yankee Stadium again. And oh yeah: The Yankees won the next five World Series, still a record.

GRAND SLAMS TIMES THREE (VS. OAKLAND ATHLETICS, AUGUST 25, 2011)

Some people asked whether it was a football game when they heard that the Yankees had beaten Oakland 22–9. To get that many runs, a team normally needs lots of home runs. And the Bronx Bombers had five against the A's–three of them grand slams.

Yep, the Yankees became the first team with a hat trick of bases-filled homers when Robinson Cano, Russell Martin, and Curtis Granderson did it.

PERFECT POSITIONING (AT SAN FRANCISCO GIANTS, 1962 WORLD SERIES)

Of all the memorable World Series the Yankees have appeared in, seven-game series against San

Ralph Terry was the hero of Game 7 as he pitched a four-hit shutout and helped the Yankees win the 1962 title.

Francisco in 1962 stands out. The Yankees won the odd-numbered games; the Giants took the even numbers. Game 7 was played by the San Francisco Bay. Back then, pitchers often threw all nine innings, and heading into the bottom of the ninth, the Yankees' Ralph Terry had a two-hit shutout, leading 1–0 on, of all things, a run scored on a double play.

The Giants' Matty Alou led off the final inning with a bunt single. With two outs, Willie Mays doubled, and because Roger Maris was in the perfect spot in right field and had a strong arm, Alou stopped at third base.

Up came left-handed slugger Willie McCovey. Manager Ralph Houk told Terry to pitch to McCovey rather than walk him in order to face slumping right-handed hitter Orlando Cepeda. McCovey then hit a screaming line drive that second baseman Bobby Richardson, also positioned perfectly, caught for the third out—and the championship.

MURCER FOR MUNSON (VS. BALTIMORE ORIOLES, AUGUST 6, 1979)

Bobby Murcer was Thurman Munson's close friend and spoke at the Yankees catcher's funeral in Ohio on August 6, 1979. Then Murcer, another in the long line of outstanding Yankees center fielders, flew back to New York to face Baltimore.

Murcer certainly could have sat out the game, but he wanted to honor Munson, who had died in a plane crash. Honor him he did with a three-run homer and then a winning two-run single for a 5–4 win.

"I never did use that bat again. I gave it to Diana," Murcer said of Munson's widow.

Bobby Murcer salutes the fans after his game-winning single against the Baltimore Orioles in 1979.

JETER'S 3,000TH (VS. TAMPA BAY RAYS, JULY 9, 2011)

There were plenty of spectacular moments for Derek Jeter. He delivered one by getting his 3,000th career hit at Yankee Stadium. None of the great Yankees had ever done that.

Plus, Jeter's 3,000th hit was a home run into the left field bleachers.

"If I would have tried to have written it and given it to someone, I wouldn't have even bought it, to be honest with you," Jeter said. "It's just one of those special days."

PINE TAR (VS. KANSAS CITY ROYALS, JULY 24, 1983)

Kansas City Royals star George Brett came to the plate to face Goose Gossage. It was the top of the ninth inning, and the game was on the line. With two outs and his team trailing by a run, Brett homered to right field to put Kansas City ahead 5–4.

Then the fun really began.

Before Brett could round the bases, Yankees manager Billy Martin was on the field to protest. Brett's bat had too much pine tar on it, Martin said, making it too sticky. The umpires looked and agreed.

Just like that, Brett's home run was erased and he was ejected from the game. And he was not happy. Brett sprinted from the dugout screaming at the umps. "I have never seen anyone as mad as George Brett on that day," Gossage said.

The drama wasn't over. The Royals protested to the league president, who ruled in their favor. When the game resumed nearly a month later, Brett got the last laugh because the homer counted. The Royals closed out their 5–4 win in just 12 minutes.

> "I have never seen anyone as mad as George Brett on that day."
>
> –Yankees pitcher Goose Gossage

DONNIE BASEBALL GOES DEEP (JULY 1987)

Don Mattingly might be the greatest Yankee never to play in a World Series. He joined the team in 1982, a year after the Yankees won the AL. He left in 1995, a year before they won the Series.

A spotless fielder at first base (nine Gold Gloves), a clutch hitter with a picture-perfect swing (.307 career average), and a team captain for five seasons, Mattingly led the league in hits, doubles, RBIs, and batting average at different times. And in 1987, he went on a home run tear with 10 in eight consecutive games.

MAZEROSKI'S HOMER (AT PITTSBURGH PIRATES, 1960 WORLD SERIES)

Imagine outscoring your opponent 46–17 through six World Series games and still having to play a deciding Game 7. It happened to the Yankees in 1960. And the seventh game was one of the best in Series history.

New York's ace pitcher Whitey Ford had won Game 6, so Bob Turley started Game 7 in Pittsburgh—and lasted just one inning. Soon, the Yankees trailed the Pirates 4–0. But they rallied with a solo homer by Moose Skowron in the fifth and four runs in the sixth, thanks mostly to Yogi Berra's three-run shot.

New York's lead became 7–4 in the eighth. With the bullpen pitching so well, the Yankees seemed headed for a championship. Then it all fell apart.

Bill Virdon's ground ball to shortstop should have been a double play, but it took a bad hop and hit Tony Kubek in the throat. He left the game with men on first and second. Soon the Pirates had gotten within a run, and then backup catcher Hal Smith sent a shot over Berra's head and into the stands.

Pittsburgh led 9–7, but the Yankees weren't done. Mickey Mantle singled in one run and then made a base-running move that, at the time, saved the Yankees. When Berra grounded out to first baseman Rocky Nelson, Mantle reversed direction and headed back to first. Nelson missed the tag that would have ended the game while Gil McDougald scooted home from third base to tie it 9–9.

Ralph Terry took the mound in the seesaw battle, and Pittsburgh's Bill Mazeroski came up. Mazeroski swung at the second pitch and, like Smith, sent it deep to left field. Berra, again, could only watch it go over his head and into the Forbes Field stands.

Mazeroski remains the only player to hit a Game 7 World Series walk-off homer.

CHAMBLISS DELIVERS A PENNANT (VS. ROYALS, 1976 ALCS)

After going through a string of poor seasons, the Yankees were ready for the big time again in 1976. They won the AL East but needed to get past Kansas City to reach the World Series. The ALCS went to a deciding fifth game. And after George Brett's three-run homer for the Royals tied the score 6–6 in the eighth, it all came down to the ninth inning.

Yankees first baseman Chris Chambliss led off the bottom of the ninth. He didn't wait, slamming Mark Littell's first pitch over the right field fence to win the pennant. Chambliss's biggest challenge came next: trying to make his way through dozens of fans who had run onto the field as he circled the bases. He even collided with a few before pouncing on home plate.

THE NO-NOS

Anytime a pitcher throws a complete game without allowing any hits, fans take notice. The Yankees' 11 no-hitters don't come close to the Dodgers' Major League Baseball (MLB) record of 26. Still, some of the no-nos are among baseball's most famous games.

At the top of that list is Don Larsen's perfecto in the 1956 World Series.

In Game 5, with the Series tied 2–2, Larsen faced 27 Dodgers and retired them all, striking out seven. Dodgers pinch-hitter Dale Mitchell fanned for the final out at Yankee Stadium. Catcher Yogi Berra ran to the mound and jumped into Larsen's arms, wrapping his legs around the pitcher. A picture of it is in the Library of Congress in Washington, DC.

"I was so nervous I couldn't think straight," Larsen said. "Yogi had to do my thinking for me."

It wasn't until 1983 that another Yankee threw a no-hitter: Dave Righetti, their future closer, did it to the Red Sox on July 4.

Ten years later came one of baseball's most special achievements. Left-hander Jim Abbott, who was born without a right hand, no-hit Cleveland.

"I had these huge goose bumps on my forearms, and the hair on the back of my neck was standing up," Don Mattingly told *Sports Illustrated*. "Maybe that would have happened with someone else. Maybe I'd have the same feelings. But I think because it was Jim there was a little something extra."

Dwight Gooden didn't allow any hits to Seattle in 1996. David Wells and David Cone each matched Larsen's perfect game, though they did it in the regular season in 1998 and 1999.

Yankees catcher Yogi Berra jumps into Don Larsen's arms after Larsen's perfect game in the 1956 World Series.

Allie Reynolds is the only Yankee who has thrown two no-hitters. In fact, both games happened in the same season. In 1951, Reynolds no-hit Cleveland in July and Boston in September.

Reynolds was one of the Yankees' top pitchers from 1947 to 1954, and in '51 he went 17–8 with an AL-high seven shutouts. He even finished third in MVP voting.

How great was his double no-hit feat in one season? Only four other pitchers have done it in MLB history.

CHAPTER 8

BASEBALL'S BITTEREST RIVALRY

Rangers fans hate the Bruins. Knicks fans despise the Celtics. Jets and Giants fans can't stand the Patriots. Forget all that. The bitterest rivalry between New York and Boston is Yankees–Red Sox. And it dates back more than a century.

The teams first met on May 7, 1903, when the New York Highlanders lost 6–2 to the Boston Americans. Since then, they've played more than 2,000 times, with the Yankees winning approximately 55 percent. Although there's a level of respect between the Sox and Yanks, there's also a stream of nastiness in baseball's greatest rivalry. And throughout all of the twists and turns were some of the game's most iconic players.

The Yankees–Red Sox rivalry went up a notch in 2004 when Alex Rodriguez joined the Bronx Bombers instead of the Sox.

THE CURSE OF THE BAMBINO

For all intents and purposes, the Yankees–Red Sox rivalry began before the 1920 season. Up to that point, Boston had all the bragging rights. The Red Sox had won five World Series to the Yankees' zero. Boston also featured some of the brightest young stars in the game. Then they sold one of them to the Yankees.

For decades, Boston fans regretted the sale of Babe Ruth to the Yankees, calling it the "Curse of the Bambino." The name made reference to Ruth's nickname, "the Bambino," which is Italian for "child."

It was bad enough that the greatest slugger in baseball history escaped from their team and went to the enemy. Ruth ended up hitting more homers than the entire Red Sox roster in 10 different seasons. And his first home run as a Yankee came against, yep, Boston. Something else happened after the trade, too. Suddenly the Yankees started winning World Series, while the once-dominant Red Sox kept falling short.

Anytime something bad happened to the Red Sox, people would wonder if the team was cursed. And in 1986, when Boston lost the World Series to another New York team, the Mets, *New York Times* columnist George Vecsey blamed the "Curse of the Bambino."

Fans of the Red Sox and Yankees have argued for decades who was better: Ted Williams or Joe DiMaggio?

JOE D. AND TEDDY BALLGAME

Which great outfielder and hitter was better, the Yankees' Joe DiMaggio or the Red Sox's Ted Williams? Both sides had plenty of ammunition, because Joe D. and Teddy Ballgame were among history's best.

In 1941 alone, Williams hit .406—no one has batted .400 since—yet DiMaggio won AL MVP honors because he had a 56-game hitting streak, a mark also unapproached since.

There's a famous story, perhaps true, perhaps not, that the team owners once met to discuss trading DiMaggio for Williams. They reasoned that with Fenway Park's short left field wall (the Green Monster), righty-hitting DiMaggio could set home run records. And with Yankee Stadium's short porch in right field, Williams could do the same.

Thankfully, it never happened, and both players became legends in their cities. DiMaggio batted .334 with 46 homers against the Red Sox, and Williams hit .345 with 62 homers against the Yankees.

PLAYING TOUGH

These incidents happened three years apart, but no matter. They equally spiced the rivalry.

The Yankees' Thurman Munson and the Sox's Carlton Fisk were All-Star catchers and heroes to their fan bases. They didn't think highly of each other. That showed one day in 1973.

Munson was on third base in a 2–2 game when Gene Michael tried to bunt, but missed. Munson kept coming, and Fisk was waiting at the plate with the ball—except Michael, who was 30 pounds lighter than

Fisk, didn't get out of the batter's box, blocking Fisk. Then Munson collided with Fisk and fell atop him. Fisk kicked him off because there were other runners on base to deal with.

So Munson threw a punch.

Others rushed in to break it up, but Michael wasn't done. He jumped Fisk from behind and began scratching and punching. That led to more brawling, including Yankees manager Ralph Houk.

Munson and Fisk were ejected, but not Michael, which made the Red Sox furious. Their revenge was winning the game in the bottom of the ninth.

In 1976, the Yankees and Fisk were at it again. Lou Piniella was racing home in the sixth inning with host New York leading 1–0. The throw from right field beat him, so Piniella barreled into the Red Sox's catcher. Fisk held on to the ball, then dived onto Piniella and began punching him.

In the midst of the bodies, New York third baseman Graig Nettles got into it with Boston left-hander Bill "Spaceman" Lee, who had insulted the Yankees after the 1973 fight. That was no contest as Lee separated his shoulder, sidelining him for much of the season—a season in which the Yankees won the pennant.

BUCKY DENT

For Yankees fans, nothing in the rivalry tops the 1978 playoff game at Fenway Park. For Red Sox fans, nothing is more painful.

New York had chased Boston most of the summer, from 14 games behind, and caught the Red Sox by sweeping four September games at Fenway. The Yankees dominated the series, outscoring their rivals by a total score of 42–9.

That sweep prompted broadcaster Tony Kubek, a former Yankees shortstop, to say: "This is the first time I've seen a first-place team chasing a second-place team."

A few weeks later, the Yankees and Red Sox finished the regular schedule tied. So the teams headed up to Boston for a one-game showdown, with Yankees ace Ron Guidry facing former Yankee Mike Torrez.

Some big stars came through at the plate. Red Sox great Carl Yastrzemski homered. So did New York's Reggie Jackson. Mickey Rivers and Thurman Munson had doubles for the Yankees. But New York trailed 2–0 in the top of the seventh. Then Chris Chambliss and Roy White singled. Up stepped shortstop Bucky Dent, hardly a power hitter.

Bucky Dent hits the home run that breaks the Red Sox's hearts in the 1978 playoff game at Fenway Park.

Dent fouled a ball off his foot and was in serious pain. But with no other infielders on the bench, he had the foot sprayed by the trainer to numb it. That's when Rivers noticed Dent's bat was cracked.

"The next thing I know, the bat boy comes up to me, takes one bat out of my hand and gives me a new bat," Dent said. "Apparently, he also delivered a message from Mickey, who told him to tell me that I was going to hit a home run with the new bat, but

BUCKY DENT

No one has more connection to the greatest baseball rivalry than Bucky Dent. He was a good shortstop who came to the Yankees from the White Sox in 1977. The next season, 1978, was one of his lesser seasons as he hit only .243, though he excelled in the field.

It took just that one swing at Fenway Park to make Dent royalty in the Bronx and a villain in New England. His dramatic home run was just his fifth of the season. It did, however, spark him to the best World Series of his life, when Dent was MVP as the Yankees beat the Los Angeles Dodgers in six games.

I wasn't paying attention to anything he was saying. The last thing I was thinking about was hitting a home run. I was just trying to get ready for the next pitch."

In came the pitch–and out it went, over the Green Monster.

Fenway fell silent. The Yankees led 3–2 and would hold on for a 5–4 victory, with closer Goose Gossage getting Yastrzemski to pop out to end it.

Yet another Yankees celebration and Red Sox failure.

AARON BOONE

If Bucky Dent is the most despised Yankee in Beantown, Aaron Boone has to be a close second. Boone's role in the rivalry was more dramatic, too. What could be more dramatic than Game 7 of the 2003 ALCS between the Red Sox and Yankees?

Boston jumped to a 4–0 lead before New York came back. The Yankees' Jason Giambi hit two solo homers, but the Red Sox got another run in the eighth, and with ace Pedro Martinez on the mound, things looked safe for Boston.

Except there's no such thing as safe in this rivalry.

Martinez weakened, and Bernie Williams drove in Derek Jeter to make it 5–3. Boston manager Grady Little left the tiring Martinez on the mound, and the pitcher gave up hits to Hideki Matsui and Jorge Posada to tie it as the Bronx ballpark quaked from the noise.

Still, the game was just tied.

Yankees manager Joe Torre had no choice but to bring in closer Mariano Rivera in the ninth and stick with him. Usually, Rivera would throw one inning and have one job: maintain the lead. In this win-or-else setting, he went three innings, allowing two hits.

The Yankees' Aaron Boone celebrates his walk-off, series-winning home run against the Red Sox in the 2003 playoffs.

The Yankees were rewarded in the 11th, adding to the "Curse of the Bambino."

Boston's Tim Wakefield delivered a knuckleball that, well, didn't knuckle. Boone sent it into the left field stands, raising both arms in triumph as he left the batter's box.

"Derek told me sometimes the ghosts show up here," Boone said. "When I joined the Yankees, this is the kind of thing I thought I could be a part of. This is the perfect story ending for everyone–extra innings in Game 7 after a comeback. It's the perfect ending."

RED SOX RALLY

After years of torment for Red Sox fans, the 2003 ALCS might have been the low point. In Game 3 of that series, Martinez hit a Yankees player with a pitch, only for Yankees pitcher Roger Clemens to throw high at a Sox slugger.

The benches cleared, and Martinez, wearing his warm-up jacket, then challenged one of the Yankees: the 72-year-old coach Don Zimmer, who fell to the ground. It was an ugly scene, and after Boone's walk-off home run in Game 7 the Sox were left with an ugly taste in their mouths.

That taste remained into the 2004 season.

Things got especially ugly on July 24 at Fenway Park, when Boston's Bronson Arroyo hit Alex Rodriguez with a pitch. As A-Rod walked toward first base, he angrily shouted at Arroyo and challenged catcher Jason Varitek to fight. So Varitek shoved his glove in Rodriguez's face, and punches flew. Both benches emptied.

Red Sox fans were so proud of Varitek that, according to ESPN, a picture of the brawl "hangs in sports bars, restaurants, and man caves all over New England."

In Boston, the moment was a welcome release after decades of frustration. In New York, it was business as usual, especially after the Yankees took a 3–0 lead in that year's ALCS. Through those three games, they outscored the Red Sox 32–16. According to baseball history, the Yankees were well on their way to a second straight World Series, once again ending their rivals' season in the process.

The Yankees were on the verge of a sweep, leading 4–3 at Fenway Park in the ninth. Yankees fans already were thinking about World Series tickets. Then the usually untouchable Rivera gave up a run. When David "Big Papi" Ortiz homered in the 12th, Boston was alive.

Very much alive.

The Red Sox took the fifth game 5–4 in 14 innings. Again, New York blew a lead, this time in the eighth. Boston had all the momentum and won Game 6 at Yankee Stadium, 4–2.

Suddenly, it looked like the Yankees were jinxed. Where were the big hits, the shut-down pitching, the great defense? All gone. Game 7 wasn't even close. The Red Sox scored six runs in the first two innings on the way to a 10–3 romp. Boston became the only baseball team to rally from three games down to win a postseason series. Of course, the Red Sox went on to win their first World Series in 86 years, too.

KELLY VS. AUSTIN

After a few years of peace, the fires were stoked with yet another brawl. Two weeks into the 2018 season, the Yankees and Red Sox went at it.

The drama began in the third inning. Yankees designated hitter Tyler Austin spiked Boston's Brock Holt on the leg while sliding into second base. The players yelled at each other as teammates stepped out of the dugout.

Then, in the seventh inning, Austin was hit by reliever Joe Kelly's 98 mph pitch. Austin

Tensions are always high when the Yankees and Red Sox play, as was evident during their 2018 brawl.

slammed his bat on home plate and took a few steps toward the mound. Kelly motioned for him to keep coming, and they fought. Others from both sides pushed and shoved. Both players were ejected, as was Yankees third base coach Phil Nevin and reliever Tommy Kahnle. Kelly wound up with a six-game suspension, and Austin received five games.

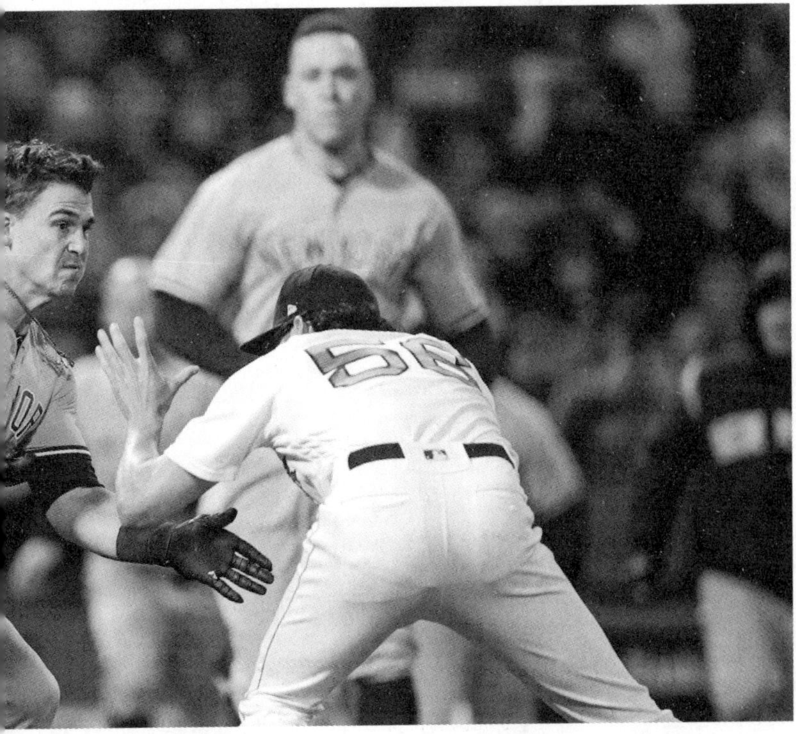

"I was ready to defend myself," Kelly said. "Someone comes on my property and in my backyard—I've got two dogs, and if you come on my property and I feel like I was getting attacked, then I'm going to have to defend myself."

CHAPTER 9

YANKEES MOUNT RUSHMORE

A Mount Rushmore for all the Yankees who truly deserve a face carving would require an entire mountain range. Unfortunately, we get only four choices. Here are the best of the best.

BABE RUTH (1920–1934)

George Herman Ruth wasn't just baseball's greatest home run hitter. He also collected some wonderful nicknames along the way. Mostly known as Babe—a nickname that went back to his school days—he was also called "The Sultan of Swat," "The King of Crash," "The Colossus of Clout," and "The Great Bambino."

Though his career ended in 1935, Babe Ruth is still regarded as one of baseball's greatest players of all time.

Ruth was originally a left-handed pitcher and outfielder for the Boston Red Sox. He won three World Series in Boston, but he wanted to be an outfielder, not a pitcher. Plus, he believed that he was underpaid. So Red Sox owner Harry Frazee sold his rights to the Yankees in January 1920 for $100,000 and a $300,000 loan. That deal would haunt Boston for the next 86 years. Whereas the Yankees were winning more than two dozen World Series, the Red Sox won zero until 2004.

While still with the Red Sox in 1918, Ruth led the majors with 11 homers. That was during baseball's "Dead Ball Era," when pitchers were allowed to scuff the ball or even throw "spitballs." Those tricks were soon banned as team owners realized fans wanted more scoring and more long balls. No one was better at hitting them far than the Babe.

In 1919, he hit 29 as a Red Sox outfielder/pitcher. The next season, as a Yankee, he hit a record 54 homers. Next best was George Sisler with 19. From there, the hefty Ruth—listed as 6 feet 2 inches, 215 pounds, but probably weighing more—won the home run title nine more times, including his record-setting 60 in 1927.

Ruth also led the AL in RBIs five times, runs scored eight times, and walks 11 times. His career batting average was .342, and despite his size, he knew how to move on the base paths. His arm was strong, naturally, and he was among baseball's best right fielders. He also won four more World Series with the Yankees.

The Babe possibly could have made the Hall of Fame as a pitcher–his record was 94–46 with a 2.28 ERA. But instead, he became the sport's most powerful slugger. In 1936, the Hall's first year, only Ty Cobb drew a higher percentage of votes than Ruth's 95.1.

Babe was as big a star as America had. He appeared in movies. He was idolized by children everywhere. He was popular in high society, and was often seen away from the field wearing a fur coat and smoking a cigar.

When anyone mentioned "The Babe" in the 1920s and '30s, there was only one person they meant: Babe Ruth.

LOU GEHRIG (1923–1939)

"Today, I consider myself the luckiest man on the face of the Earth."

Maybe the most famous words in any baseball speech, the "Iron Horse" said them at Yankee Stadium when he was honored on July 4, 1939, two weeks

Lou Gehrig was baseball's original iron man as he played in 2,130 consecutive games.

after the great first baseman retired. He was struck with ALS, which became known as Lou Gehrig's disease, and would die two years later.

Gehrig showed up for work every day for an incredible 2,130 straight games. He was part of the Yankees' "Murderer's Row," wearing No. 4 and usually batting behind Ruth, who wore No. 3. And while Ruth was the home run king, Gehrig wasn't far behind as he helped lead the team to eight World Series.

A native of New York City, Gehrig actually was shy and not all that sure he could make it in the big leagues. But make it Gehrig did, replacing Yankees first baseman Wally Pipp in June 1925 and staying in the lineup every game for 14 straight years.

In 1931, Gehrig had one of the best seasons in baseball history: 211 hits, 163 runs scored, 46 home runs, 185 RBIs, and a .341 batting average. Overall, Gehrig had a .340 career batting average, with 493 homers.

Gehrig, also a strong fielder and team leader, was once described by the *New York Times* as the "idol of cheering millions."

Like Ruth, Gehrig entered the Hall of Fame.

JOE DIMAGGIO (1936–1951) (DNP 1943–45 DUE TO MILITARY SERVICE)

DiMaggio was once called "the greatest ballplayer I ever saw" by his biggest rival, Ted Williams.

"Joltin' Joe" even had songs written about him and was married to glamorous actress Marilyn Monroe. *Sporting News* ranked the center fielder,

Joe DiMaggio wowed the fans in 1941 when he recorded a hit in 56 consecutive games.

who wore No. 5, as the 11th greatest player in baseball history. Gehrig was sixth and Ruth was first.

DiMaggio, whose brothers Dom and Vince also played in the majors, missed three seasons while serving in the Army. Yet he won two batting, home run, and RBI crowns; won three AL MVP Awards; and was selected for the All-Star Game in each of his 13 seasons. His career batting average was .325, and the Yankees won nine World Series with him.

Most impressive of all was DiMaggio's 56-game hitting streak in 1941. No one in the modern era has come within 10 games of that record. And after DiMaggio went hitless at Cleveland on July 17—third baseman Ken Keltner robbed him of two hits with spectacular defensive plays—the "Yankee Clipper" hit safely in his next 16 contests.

"There is always some kid who may be seeing me for the first or last time, I owe him my best," DiMaggio said of his consistency.

A good measure of DiMaggio's brilliance: In 1949, he became the first baseball player to be paid $100,000 in a season. And in 1955 he joined Ruth and Gehrig in the Hall of Fame.

DEREK JETER (1995–2014)

When Jeter joined the Yankees in 1995 as a rookie, they hadn't won the World Series in 17 years. The team often traded away young players for veteran stars during those seasons, and it led to weak records.

Jeter was different. The Yankees knew what they had: a shortstop who could hit and field with the very best. A leader. A clutch performer.

Derek Jeter's decorated career included a World Series MVP Award in 2000 as he led the Yankees to a win over the rival Mets in five games.

Their faith in Jeter paid off with five championships.

"If you're going to play at all, you're out to win," he said. "Baseball, board games, playing Jeopardy, I hate to lose."

For 20 years, Jeter was the big man in the Bronx. Eight times, he had more than 200 hits in a season, twice leading the league. His lifetime average was .310.

Jeter made the All-Star team in 14 of his 20 major league seasons. He earned five Gold Gloves for his fielding. In 2000, when the Yankees beat the crosstown rival Mets in the World Series, Jeter was MVP.

He was the top guy in the Core Four that also included pitchers Mariano Rivera and Andy Pettitte and catcher Jorge Posada. In the toughest spots in a town where winning is everything, his teammates usually turned to Jeter. He produced.

"It was an honor and a privilege to play with Derek for so many years," Rivera said. "He was all about winning, and it was something special to see how he conducted himself on and off the field. He can teach a lot of youngsters, by example, about how to play the game."

THE BEST OF THE REST

YOGI BERRA (1946–63; 1964, 1984–85 MANAGER)

No one has won more baseball championships than the former catcher and outfielder, who later managed the team. He won 10 World Series, one ahead of Yankees teammate Joe DiMaggio.

EARLE COMBS (1924–35)

Sometimes forgotten while playing on a Yankees dynasty with Babe Ruth and Lou Gehrig, outfielder Combs batted .325 in 12 seasons and led the 1927 Yankees–considered the best team ever–in hits.

BILL DICKEY (1928–43, 1946)

The catcher was an 11-time All-Star who had a .313 career batting average and three times led the AL in throwing out base stealers.

WHITEY FORD (1950, 1953–67)

A left-hander with such a collection of pitches that batters never knew what was coming, Ford won 10 World Series games and 236 in the regular season.

TONY LAZZERI (1926–37)

A man for all positions in the infield on some of the best teams in baseball history, Lazzeri played second base, third, and shortstop.

MICKEY MANTLE (1951–68)

A Triple Crown winner in 1956 (led the league in homers, RBIs, and batting average), Mantle was a switch-hitting power center fielder with speed and excellent defense.

JOE MCCARTHY (1931–46)

Along with Casey Stengel, McCarthy is the career leader in World Series titles for a manager with seven.

MARIANO RIVERA (1995–2013)

The greatest relief pitcher, Rivera finished his 19-year career with a record 652 saves. Rivera also dominated in the postseason.

PHIL RIZZUTO (1941–42, 1946–56)

"Scooter" was the glue of many championship teams, the 1950 AL MVP, and a five-time All-Star shortstop.

RED RUFFING (1930–42, 1945–46)

Ruffing won at least 14 games in 12 seasons and was also a good pinch hitter.

CASEY STENGEL (1949–60)

"The Old Professor" was 1,149–696 and tied Joe McCarthy with seven world titles as manager.

TIMELINE

1903

The team that becomes the Yankees begins play in New York.

1912

Pinstripes first appear on the team's uniforms. One year later, the team changes names from the Highlanders to the Yankees.

1920

Babe Ruth is bought from the Red Sox and hits a record 54 home runs. One year later, the Yankees win their first AL pennant.

1923

Yankee Stadium opens with a 4–1 win over the Red Sox before a reported crowd of 74,200. Later in the year, the Yankees win their first World Series.

1927

Ruth sets the record for home runs in a season with 60. The Yankees win the World Series.

1929

The Yankees become the first team to make numbers a permanent part of the uniform.

1932

Ruth supposedly calls his own shot, predicting a home run, and the Yankees sweep the World Series from the Cubs.

1936

Joe DiMaggio joins the Yankees, and they win the first of four straight championships.

1939

After playing in a record 2,130 consecutive games, Lou Gehrig's playing streak ends due to illness. His uniform No. 4 is the first to be retired in MLB.

1941

DiMaggio has a record 56-game hitting streak, and the Yankees win another World Series.

1949

The Yankees begin a string of five straight World Series titles, which is still a record.

1956

Don Larsen pitches the only perfect game in World Series history, a 2–0 win over Brooklyn, as the Yankees win another title.

1961

Roger Maris hits his 61st home run in the season's final game to pass Ruth's record. But he does so in a 162-game season, whereas Ruth played in a 154-game season in 1927.

1973

George Steinbrenner buys the team from CBS.

1977

Reggie Jackson hits three home runs in Game 6 of the World Series as the Yankees defeat the Dodgers.

1978

Ron Guidry sets a team record by striking out 18 batters in one game. Billy Martin resigns as manager. Despite being 14 games back in the standings at one point, Bob Lemon leads the team into a playoff with Boston, which New York wins 5–4 as Bucky Dent hits a three-run homer. The Yankees then beat the Dodgers again to win their second World Series in a row.

1996

Champions again: New York wins its first World Series since 1978.

1998

The Yankees set an AL record with their 112th win of the season on their way to the first of three straight World Series titles.

2004

The Curse of the Bambino ends as Boston wins four straight playoff games after falling behind in games 3–0. The Yankees become the first team to blow a 3–0 lead in a series.

2009

The new Yankee Stadium opens across the street from the old one. The Yankees go on to win their 27th World Series by defeating the Philadelphia Phillies in six games.

2011

Jeter gets his 3,000th career hit, the first Yankee to do it with a home run. Rivera sets a major league record for career saves with his 602nd.

2018

With a 100–62 record, the Yankees have their 26th consecutive season with a winning record.

YANKEES RECORDS

ALL-TIME RECORD

10,275–7,781

PLAYOFFS RECORD

98–74

WORLD SERIES RECORD

134–90–1

CAREER BATTING LEADER

Babe Ruth: .349

CAREER HOME RUNS LEADER

Babe Ruth: 659

CAREER RBIs LEADER

Lou Gehrig: 1,995

CAREER PITCHING WINS LEADER

Whitey Ford: 236

CAREER SAVES LEADER

Mariano Rivera: 652

CAREER STOLEN BASES LEADER

Derek Jeter: 358

WINNINGEST MANAGER

Joe McCarthy: 1,460–867

**Accurate through the 2018 season.*

FOR MORE INFORMATION

BOOKS

Castro, Tony. *Gehrig & the Babe: The Friendship and the Feud*. Chicago: Triumph Books, 2018.

Fischer, David. *Aaron Judge: The Incredible Story of the New York Yankees' Home Run-Hitting Phenom*. New York: Sports Publishing, 2017.

Frommer, Harvey. *Red Sox vs. Yankees: The Great Rivalry*. Lanham, MD: Taylor Trade Publishing, 2014.

ON THE WEB

Baseball Reference
www.baseball-reference.com

Major League Baseball
www.mlb.com

New York Yankees
www.mlb.com/yankees

PLACES TO VISIT

NATIONAL BASEBALL HALL OF FAME AND MUSEUM

25 Main Street

Cooperstown, NY 13326

888-425-5633

www.baseballhall.org

Learn about baseball's greatest players of all time as well as the history of America's pastime through exhibits and artifacts.

YANKEE STADIUM

1 East 161st Street

Bronx, NY 10451

212-926-5337

www.mlb.com/yankees/ballpark

Next door to where the original "House That Ruth Built" once stood, the new Yankee Stadium maintains the same general look of the original as well as features such as Monument Park. The ballpark also includes a Yankees museum.

SELECT BIBLIOGRAPHY

"61 Home Runs by Roger Maris." *Baseball Almanac*, www.baseball-almanac.com/feats/feats12b.shtml. Accessed 8 Aug. 2018.

Corcoran, Cliff. "99 Cool Facts about Babe Ruth." *Sports Illustrated*, 11 July 2013, www.si.com/mlb/strike-zone/2013/07/12/99-cool-facts-about-babe-ruth.

Matthews, Wallace. "Aaron Judge Leads the Renewed Bronx Bombers Past the Orioles." *New York Times*, 29 April 2017, https://nyti.ms/2qjBts7.

McCarron, Anthony. "It's the Curse of Boonebino! Aaron Boone Homers in the 11th to Beat the Red Sox in the 2003 ALCS." *New York Daily News*, 16 Oct. 2015, www.nydailynews.com/sports/baseball/yankees/curse-boonebinoshot-11th-history-sox-article-1.518448.

McDonald, Joe. "Varitek/A-Rod Brawl, 10 Years Later." ESPN.*com*, 24 July 2014, www.espn.com/boston/mlb/story/_/id/11256420/2004-boston-red-sox-new-york-yankees-brawl-remember-starring-jason-varitek-alex-rodriguez.

Nightengale, Bob. "Derek Jeter's Unbelievable Closing Act at Yankee Stadium." USA *Today*, 26 Sept. 2014, http://usat.ly/1pfoTBL.

Robinson, Ray. "Lou Gehrig: Columbia Legend and American Hero." *Living Legacies*, www.columbia.edu/cu/alumni/Magazine/Fall2001/Gehrig.html. Accessed 8 Aug. 2018.

Santasiere, Alfred, III. "Yankees Magazine: A Monster moment." *MLB.com*, 31 Aug. 2016, https://atmlb.com/2vcHgE1.

INDEX

Arroyo, Luis, 41, 43–44
Atlanta Braves, 58

Baker, Frank "Home Run," 13
Baltimore Orioles, 7, 11, 35, 57–58, 65,
Berra, Yogi, 21, 23, 50, 51, 53, 67–68, 70
Boggs, Wade, 59, 61–62
Boone, Aaron, 81, 83
Boston Red Sox, 9, 13, 73–87, 90

Chesbro, Jack, 12
Chicago Cubs, 23, 30–31
Chicago White Sox, 80
Clemens, Roger, 41, 83
Cleveland Indians, 22
Combs, Earle, 15, 17, 21

Dent, Bucky, 79, 80, 81
Detroit Tigers, 51
Dickey, Bill, 23
DiMaggio, Joe, 21, 23, 26, 29, 33, 50, 75–76, 93–95

Ford, Whitey, 41, 42, 50

Gehrig, Lou, 15, 17, 21, 22, 23, 26, 29, 32–33, 50, 91–93
Girardi, Joe, 54
Gossage, Goose, 41, 44, 50, 66
Green, Dallas, 51
Gregorious, Didi, 39
Guidry, Ron, 41, 42, 60

Halas, George, 13
Henrich, Tommy, 50
Highlanders, 11–13, 23, 73
Hilltop Park, 11-12, 19
Howser, Dick, 51
Huggins, Miller, 26, 49–50
Hunter, Catfish, 41, 50

Jackson, Reggie, 27, 35–37, 50, 52–53, 80
Jeter, Derek, 5–9, 23, 24, 26–27, 54, 57, 61, 65, 81, 95–97
Judge, Aaron, 29–30, 39

Kansas City Royals, 66, 69
Keeler, Willie, 12

Larsen, Don, 69–70
Lazzeri, Tony, 15, 32
Lemon, Bob, 49, 51, 53
Los Angeles Dodgers, 36–37, 52, 69–70, 80
Lyle, Sparky, 41, 44

Mantle, Mickey, 21, 23, 26, 29, 33–34

Maris, Roger, 23, 29, 34–35, 64
Martin, Billy, 23, 49, 51–54, 66
Mattingly, Don, 67, 70
McCarthy, Joe, 49, 50
Michael, Gene, 49, 76–77
Minnesota Twins, 51
Monument Park, 26
Munson, Thurman, 64, 76–77, 80
Murcer, Bobby, 64

New York Giants (baseball), 12–13, 14–15, 19
New York Mets, 24

Oakland Athletes, 32, 35, 53, 61, 62

Pennock, Herb, 41
Pettitte, Andy, 9, 54, 97
Piniella, Lou, 49, 51, 53–54
Pittsburgh Pirates, 17, 67–68
Polo Grounds, 12–13, 15, 19–20
Posada, Jorge, 9, 54, 97

Reynolds, Allie, 71
Righetti, Dave, 44, 70
Rivera, Mariano, 9, 41, 44, 46, 54, 81, 85, 97
Rizzuto, Phil, 6, 23
Rodriguez, Alex, 29, 37–39, 46
Ruffing, Red, 50
Ruth, Babe, 13, 14–15, 17, 20, 21, 22, 23, 24, 26, 29, 30–31, 32, 34, 37, 50, 59, 74, 89–91, 92–93

Sanchez, Gary, 29, 39
San Francisco Giants, 62–64
Shea Stadium, 24
Showalter, Buck, 54
Stanton, Giancarlo, 29, 39
Steinbrenner, George, 23, 26, 49–54
Stengel, Casey, 49, 50
Sterling, John, 8

Tampa Bay Rays, 65
Terry, Ralph, 63
Texas Rangers, 51
Torre, Joe, 9, 23, 54, 81

Virdon, Bill, 51, 68

Williams, Bernie, 54

Yankee Stadium, 6, 15, 20–21, 24–27, 30, 58, 62, 85

ABOUT THE AUTHOR

Barry Wilner has been a sportswriter for the Associated Press since 1976. He covered the Yankees' Bronx Zoo in the 1970s. An adjunct professor at Manhattanville College, Barry also has authored 67 books. He lives in Garnerville, New York.